The Leprechaun Who

Lost His Luck

by Blaine Hackett
Illustrations by Miesha Hackett

In loving memory of Chris,
whose Irish eyes were always
smilin'

DEDICATION

I'm so excited to see this story published which was originally written in 2009. Ten years later, here we are! But there are so many people who had a hand in making this book a reality.

First, I dedicate this book to my kids, Casey and Sydney because without them, I would not have written any of my stories.

Next, to my wife, Sue, who has supported and encouraged me in this endeavor.

I would like to thank my niece Miesha Hackett for all the excellent illustrations. Who knew her talents were right under my nose?

Thank you also to the teachers at St. John's School of Little Canada MN especially Amy Burgoyne and Jen Loots. I am so very grateful they let me test out my stories on their classes.

Thank you to author Amanda Zieba for her mentoring and counsel. A quick conversation about writing with someone I did not know at a birthday party and the connection was made. Life is so interesting!

Steph Vallin deserves thanks for all her great edits and suggestions and my niece Jessica Hackett for her final tech edits.

A big thanks goes out to author Gary Harbo for his counsel and encouragement. If it weren't for him "The Breggin O'Shaunessy Song" would never have been made.

For their excellent musical talent thank you Alan Lecher for notating and Jeff Carlson for the ukulele accompaniment for "The Breggin O'Shaunessy Song"!

Finally, thank you to Mr. Chris Roth who's last minute graphic advice saved the day!

There once was a happy little leprechaun, named Breggin O'Shaughnessy, who lived and played in the lush, green Irish countryside. This is a story about how this leprechaun lost his luck.

You do know where leprechauns get their luck don't you? Why it's their four-leaf clover they keep in their vest pocket.

Now this little leprechaun loved to lay in the grass, play his ukulele and sing his favorite song which went something like this.

"I am a little leprechaun as lucky as can be, I laugh and dance and sing and play in fields so merrily. Kili-kee!, Kili-ka!, Kili-ki!, Killi-kum! Kili-kee!, Kili-ka!, Kili-ki!, Killi-kum!" *Music on page 33!*

And he would go on like that all day if you'd let him but like most boys, Breggin had chores to do. On this particular day though, he had finished his chores and went off to play.

4

Now Breggin was a carefree leprechaun which at times made him careless, especially with his clover. His mother told him time and again not to use his vest pocket for anything but his clover and keep the flap snapped "right tight". But he didn't listen!

Breggin skipped down to the babbling brook to catch some trout from the cool, pure water, laughing and singing as he went. When he got there, he reached into his vest pocket to pull out his fishing line. As he did, his four-leaf clover fell into the brook and was quickly carried away by the swift water.

"Oh no!" he cried. "What have I done?" He knew his mother would be very angry and was afraid to tell her but he was in a panic, so he ran all the way back to his cottage.

6

Bursting through the front door, he yelled, "Mother! Mother! Come quickly!" His mother was in the kitchen baking bread and turned with a concerned look as he ran in.

"What is it child?" she asked.

"Please don't be mad at me, Mother. Please!" he cried with tears rushing down his face.

"Well, tell me what the matter is... and then I'll decide whether to be mad or not."

"I lost it! I lost my four leafed clover in the brook. I pulled out me fishin' line and it fell in. It's gone!" he sobbed.

"Breggin O'shaughnessy!" his mother cried, as that was his name. "How many times have I told ya? Don't go usin' that pocket for anything but your clover!"

"I know, Mother. I know. What am I to do?" he said still crying.

8

"Well, ya can't go out of the cottage until we find another clover. We can't afford someone to be catchin' ya and takin away our pot-o-gold," she said sternly.

"Not go outside? That's not fair!" cried Breggin.

"Well ya should 'a thought of that before ya went and lost yer clover laddie. Now I've got to go out. You stick tight to the cottage." And at that she left, leaving Breggin all by his lonesome.

For the first few hours Breggin just sat around feeling sorry for himself. But after a while he started to feel... hungry. He decided he would make himself some lunch.

His mother had some nice rainbow trout in the fridge cooling in a bowl of water. Trout with a light coating of flour, pan fried in butter sounded like just the thing to make him feel better. He reached above the stove to get the flour and "poof" the whole tin fell right on this head.

Breggin stood there with flour sifting down his face, which now had a very disgusted look on it.

He saw a towel sitting on the counter and grabbed it with a jerk to wipe the flour off his face. But he did not see the meat hammer sitting on it.

The hammer fell from the counter and landed right on his big toe. "Ooohooohooo," he screamed, jumping around on one foot and holding his bruised big toe.

He went to sit down and completely missed the chair, falling right on his bum with an awful bang. To make matters worse, when he fell, a pitcher of honey that was on the table tipped over and poured out all over him. He sat there on the floor, covered with flour and gooey honey from head to his throbbing big toe. Just then his mother walked in.

"Breggin! What are ya doin?" she asked looking at her messy son.

"I was tryin' to get some lunch and everything just went... crazy!" he exclaimed.

"Well, what d'ya expect? You just lost your clover. When leprechauns lose their clover not only do they lose their good luck, but for a time after they have bad luck," she said.

14

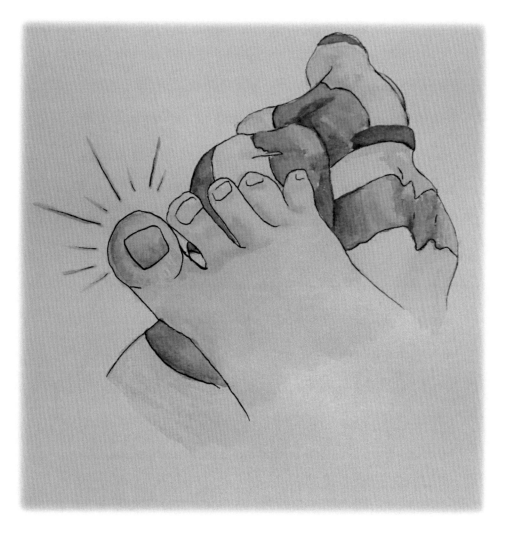

"Well that is terrible," Breggin whined smacking his hand on the floor and feeling like he was going to cry again.

"Well maybe ya've learned yer lesson. Now calm down. We'll find you a new clover. Don't worry," his mother said trying to sooth him.

But his mother ended up being very busy over the next few days and did not have time to help him. Breggin could not go out of the cottage for fear someone would catch him. This made matters worse as Mrs. O'Shaughnessy counted on Breggin to run errands which made her even busier than before.

So, Breggin fumbled around the cottage for several weeks. He broke most every clay pot his mother had and he dropped her favorite necklace down the drain.

One day he wanted to be helpful so he began making candles out of bees' wax. Everything was going fine until he tested the first one. Again, he had been told many times not to play with matches, but he thought, "I'm not playin' with em, I'm usin' em", so Breggin lit the wick on his first candle.

As the wick caught fire and gave off a wonderfully warm glow, his heart warmed and he felt he was helping his mother again. The small flame started to grow and little sparks flitted up off the end of the flame.

Suddenly and without warning the entire candle caught fire and was shooting sparks all about the living room. The rug caught fire and it was making its way to the drapes when his mother walked in, saw the fire, and calmly doused it with a large bucket of water. That was the last straw.

18

As she looked at him sternly, Breggin bowed his head. "That's it! If we don't find you a new clover, we may not have a cottage left! We are going to find you a new one first thing in the morning," she pronounced.

But, as usual, she forgot she had to be at the market first thing in the morning. Breggin could not wait. He felt horrible for his mother having to deal with all his shenanigans over the last few weeks, so that morning, he snuck out of the cottage in hopes of finding a new four leafed clover for himself.

Unfortunately for Breggin, his luck went from bad to worse when a huge, terrible man named Hamish McDougal arrived from Scotland. Hamish had a large, red beard which hung down over his huge belly. His coal black eyes sat deeply under his bushy red eyebrows and he barely had any teeth left.

Hamish had heard about the leprechauns in this part of Ireland. He was a very greedy man and wanted to catch one to get a pot-o-gold. He figured if he did, he would not have to work another day in his life. He had just sat down on a stump to rest, after a day of walking the trails in search of a leprechaun, when he saw Breggin step out of the forest into a huge field of lush, green clover.

He could not believe his luck! He had barely been in the area for a day and already he had found a leprechaun, and a none too smart leprechaun at that. As quietly as his large feet could move, Hamish snuck from tree to tree in hopes of surprising the leprechaun.

Breggin had no idea of the danger he was in. He was so intent on finding a four leafed clover that he didn't even hear the clumsy footsteps of the Scotsman coming up behind him.

However, Hamish was as smelly as he was lazy. Breggin got a whiff of something that smelled of old moldy cheese. He stood up and looked behind him. What he saw made him freeze for a split second.

The large, lumbering man was rushing toward him. Breggin came out of his trance just in time and took off running as fast as his little legs could carry him. Even though he was a fast leprechaun, one of Hamish's strides covered ten of Breggin's.

He heard an awful laugh behind him and knew he was in deep trouble. "Ah ha! Now I've got ch'a, ya wee, little leprechaun. I'll be taking that gold from ya now." Hamish yelled as he ran up behind Breggin.

What would Breggin do? He had to tell any-one who caught him where their pot of gold was. That was the rule. What would his mother say? What would she do?

As Breggin came out onto the path running as fast as he could, he looked behind him to see Hamish right on his heels. He kicked it into high gear and started to pull ahead of the Scotsman when his toe caught on a rock in the path and he went sprawling onto his belly.

And that's when he saw it. As he pulled his nose out of the dirt, he saw a single clover pop-ping up out of the trail... and it had four leaves. As quick as a whip, he pulled the clover out of the ground, bounced up and faced Hamish McDougal.

Well, Hamish was so surprised by the lepre-chaun's actions, he tried to stop his incredible for-ward momentum.

Unfortunately for him the weight of his large belly would not allow him to stop. Hamish stumbled forward and caught his toe on the same rock Breggin had. The rock upended him and he flew through the air... right into Farmer Hannigan's pig pen next to the road.

Hamish McDougal, fell, face first into the stinky mess where the pigs had just been fed their morning slop. He screamed in anger but when he turned to find the leprechaun, all that was left was a tiny puff of dust in the middle of the trail.

Breggin ran all the way home to tell his mother. And although she was very cross that he left the cottage by himself, once she had heard of his narrow escape and finding of new four leaf clover, she forgot how angry she was.

She pulled him close to her, hugging him like she would never let him go.

And from that day forward, Breggin never put anything else but his clover in his vest pocket and made sure that the flap was snapped 'right tight'!

The End

Thank you so much for reading *The Leprechaun Who Lost His Luck*!

This story was inspired by my love of all things Irish! The songs and stories are mysterious and festive. The people are warm and inviting and of course the accent... who doesn't love an Irish accent?

Please watch for more of my stories coming soon!

The Lazy Little Easter Bunny

The Cupid Who Couldn't Shoot Straight

The Little Red Schoolhouse

And more!

For more information about me and my stories please visit **blainehackett.com**

Break out the *ukulele* and give this song a go!

32979437R00021

Made in the USA
Lexington, KY
07 March 2019